BOOK THREE

A Story About Forgiving Others

EINSTEIN'S ENORMOUS ERROR

by SHEILA WALSH

illustrations by DON SULLIVAN

A CHILDREN OF FAITH BOOK *published by* WATERBROOK PRESS

EINSTEIN'S ENORMOUS ERROR
PUBLISHED BY WATERBROOK PRESS
2375 Telstar Drive, Suite 160
Colorado Springs, Colorado 80920
A division of Random House, Inc.

ISBN 1-57856-335-6

Published in association with the literary agency of Alive Communications, Inc.,
7680 Goddard Street, Suite 200, Colorado Springs, CO 80920.

The executive producer of Gnoo Zoo is Stephen Arterburn, M.Ed.
Children of Faith, 402 BNA Drive, Suite 600, Nashville, TN 37217

Library of Congress Cataloging-in-Publication Data
Walsh, Sheila.
    Einstein's enormous error : a story about forgiving others / by Sheila Walsh ;
illustrations by Don Sullivan.
        p. cm. — (Gnoo Zoo ; bk. 3)
      Summary: The carousel animals are off on another adventure but when Einstein the
elephant carelessly eats one of the tools needed to reach the True Gnoo Key, some of the
others are reluctant to forgive him.
      ISBN 1-57856-335-6
      [1. Forgiveness—Fiction. 2. Conduct of life—Fiction. 3. Merry-go-round—Fiction.] I.
Sullivan, Don, ill. II. Title. III. Series.

    PZ7.W168935 Ei 2001
    [Fic]—dc21
                                                                        2001046633

Printed in the United States of America
2001—First Edition

10 9 8 7 6 5 4 3 2 1

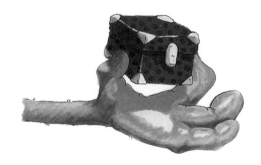

"You will only find the True Gnoo Key together," Toodaloo said.

He gave a small red box to Chattaboonga. "Take this," he said. "Now I must be off. Toodle pip!" Then he was gone.

Chattaboonga opened the box carefully. Nestled inside were four candy hammers.

"No doubt we'll need those hammers on the next part of our journey!" Big Billy said.

—*Chattaboonga's Chilling Choice*

Einstein was ready for adventure. Hammers were his kind of thing. He pretended to swing one from side to side as he and his friends tramped through the dark woods.

"Careful. Careful! You are ruffling my airspace!" Miss Marbles said.

Finally the Great White Tiger's travelers paused to rest beside a stream.

"May I hold the little box?" Einstein asked Big Billy. "I do believe I spied a note inside. It would be my pleasure to peruse it."

Big Billy smiled and nodded.

"Peruse? Well, peruse *schmooze!*" Chattaboonga said, handing over the box.

Einstein lifted the lid, and they all peeked inside.

Miss Marbles snatched the creamy pink hammer. "Look!
It matches my feathers!"

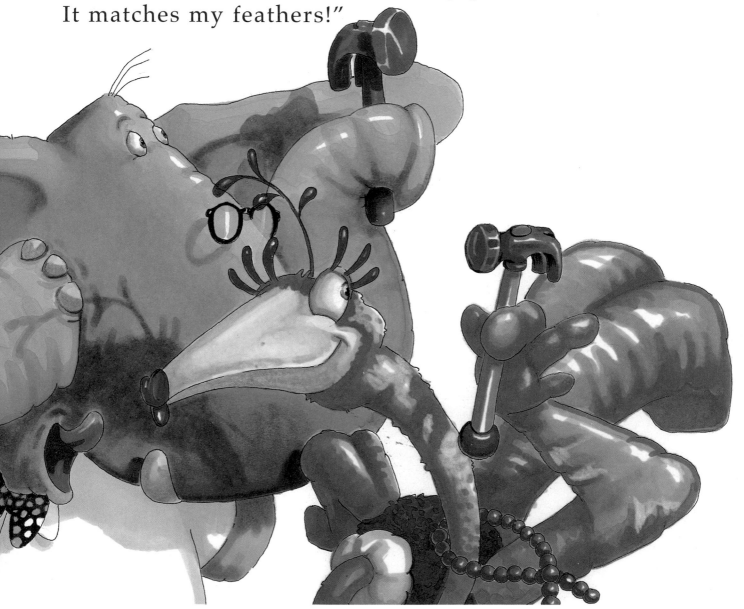

"Here, Big Billy. This is the color of your nose!" Einstein said, giving him the shiny blue-black licorice one.

Boongachatta and her sister gazed lovingly at the swirly lemon-lime hammer. "This one is cool!" she said. "It must be for us."

Einstein beamed when he saw the fourth hammer. "Chocolate! My favorite!"

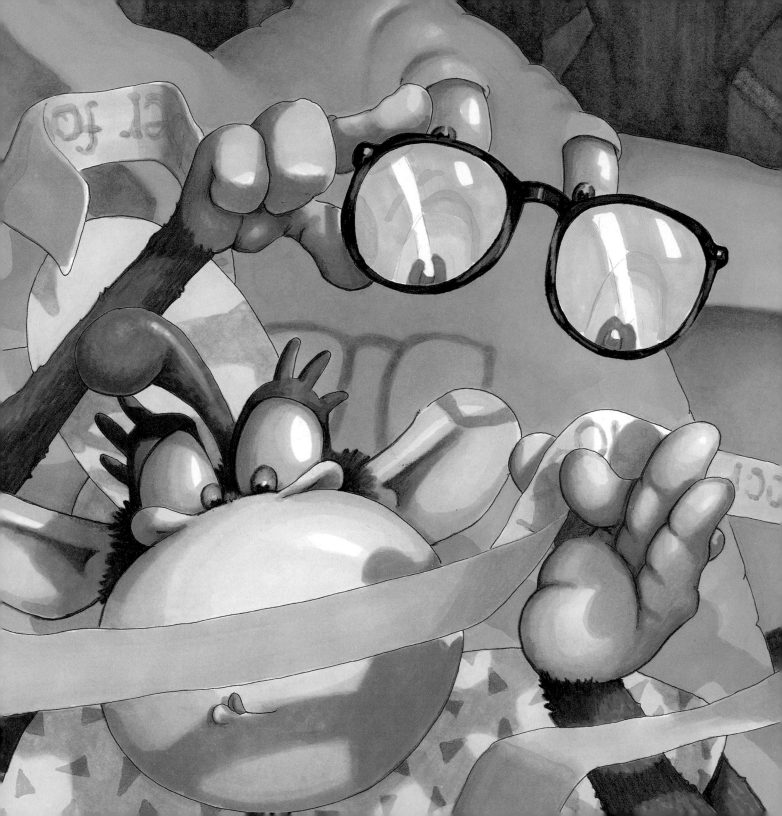

Miss Marbles interrupted Einstein's scrumptious thoughts. "There is a note," she said.

"Why don't you read it to us, Einstein?" Big Billy said.

The elephant cleared his throat. "Ahem!

'As you travel on together,
take one hammer, find its door.
Knock three times and it will open.
The True Gnoo Key's at Number Four!'"

"How exciting!" said Miss Marbles, swinging her pearls around as girls do. "We're almost there!"

Her necklace snagged Einstein's trunk and sent his glasses flying.

"Get those ooooooooffffffffff me!" he cried.

"Don't be so dramatic!" Miss Marbles said. "You big...oh...oh...overstuffed mattress!"

Einstein was so hurt that he nibbled on his chocolate hammer for comfort—but just the unimportant parts.

Miss Marbles suddenly squealed. "Look!" she cried. "Over there—a pink door in that tree. It matches my hammer!" She trotted over and tapped the door daintily.

"No, my dear Miss Marbles," Big Billy said. "*Knock* three times, remember?"

She knocked once, twice, three times—and the door swung open.

Boongachatta peered inside. "Ugh! It's dark in there."

"Einstein, would you lead us?" Big Billy asked. "We'll need your sharp eyes."

Einstein stepped through the door and paused.
   He never had liked the dark much.
      His tummy gave a nervous, elephant-size rumble.

Boongachatta screamed. "Reptillion! I heard his rumble!"

Her shriek made Einstein lose his balance. He found himself tumbling

    down

        down

           down

               a spiraling slide until he landed
                         in a heap at the bottom.

"Are you all right?" Big Billy called.

"I suppose so, no thanks to that noisy monkey! I think my hammer is cracked."

Einstein held it up for a look and noticed he was in a round room filled with mirrors.

One by one his friends whizzed down the slide.

"I'm sorry I scared you, Einstein!" Boongachatta said.

"*Humph!*" Einstein replied, turning his back on her.

Big Billy tried to smooth things over. "Einstein! Here's another door. Try your hammer."

He did. Nothing happened.

"Me now!" said Boongachatta. She knocked three times with her lemon-lime hammer and the door opened.

Einstein nibbled sadly on his chocolate hammer.

Beyond the door, a beautiful hot-air balloon rested on a sandy beach.

Everyone hurried toward it. Everyone except Einstein. He had the blues.

Big Billy found a shiny blue-black door in the side of the basket. He took out his hammer and knocked three times. The door opened. "All aboard!" he cried.

"Guess I don't need this!" Einstein said, finishing off the rest of his hammer.

I caaan't breeeeathe!

"Look!" Chattaboonga cried, pointing to a polka-dot chest sitting on the bottom of the basket. Engraved on the top were the letters

T . G . K .

"The True Gnoo Key!" Big Billy cried. "Einstein, it's your turn. Use your hammer!"

Einstein instantly felt worse than he had ever felt before.

"Come on, Einstein!" Boongachatta cried. "For you and me, just use that key!"

Come, Creepshaw. We must have that box!

Einstein twirled his bow tie nervously. "I...I...I ate it!"

"You *ate* your hammer?" everyone cried in disbelief.

"Do I detect trouble?" a voice boomed. Einstein and his friends spun around. "I think we may be of help. We are Reptiddle and Creeptiddle, locksmiths to the stars!"

"Can you open this?" Big Billy asked, holding out the box.

"Most certainly!" Reptiddle said, reaching for it.

"No!" Chattaboonga cried. "It's Reptillion! Look at his tail!"

"Hate to say this, boss, but I told you—" Creepshaw began.

"Aahhrrghh!" Reptillion roared. He swiped at Creepshaw, ripping the balloon in the process.

The wind began to blow the tattered balloon out to sea. Wild waves lapped at the basket.

"Higher, Billy, higher!" Chattaboonga cried.

"I can't! We're too heavy!" he shouted.

"Great White Tiger, help us!" everyone cried together.

"My, my, my. You *are* in a pickle!"

"Lulu!" Big Billy cried. "The Great White Tiger heard us!"

Lulu shook her brilliant mane, and a shower of sparkling snowflakes fell gently onto the balloon. In no time it was sailing safely high in the air.

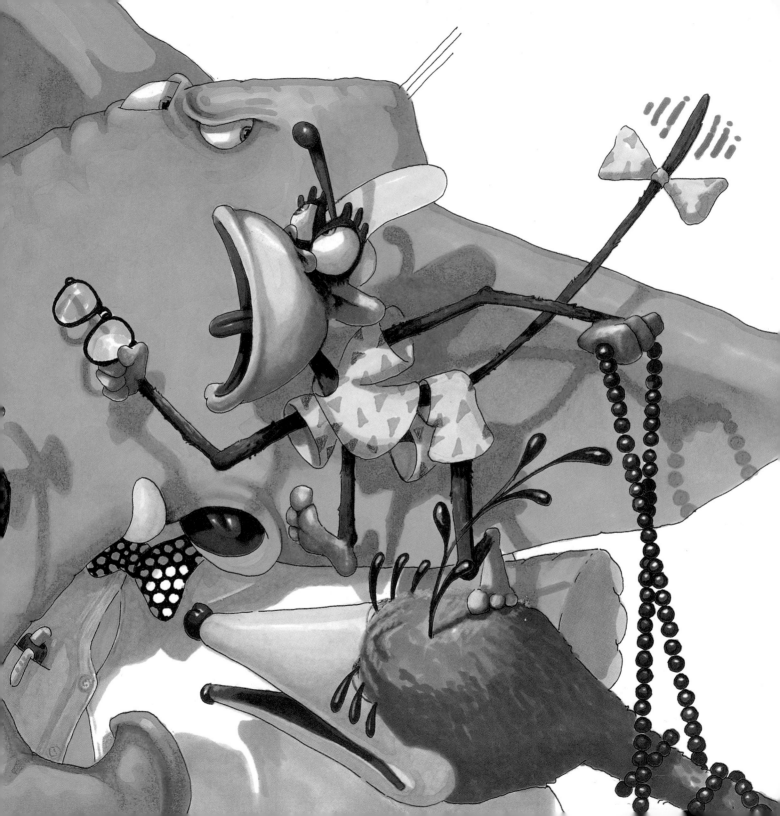

But Miss Marbles and Boongachatta were too busy arguing with Einstein to be grateful.

"This is all your fault!" Miss Marbles began. "If you weren't so touchy—"

"And greedy!" Boongachatta added.

"Well, if *you* weren't so mean," Einstein shot back, "and if *you* hadn't made me fall—"

"Now, now, now," Lulu said. "The Great White Tiger has forgiven each of you for many mistakes."

Everyone fell silent. Lulu was right.

Einstein hung his head. "I'm so sorry, everyone! Boongachatta, please forgive me for being angry."

"I forgive you!" she said, planting a big kiss on his head.

"Take my beads, Einstein. I insist!" Miss Marbles said. "I'm really quite, quite sorry!"

"I forgive you!" Einstein said.

"And we forgive you for eating your hammer," Big Billy said as he hugged his friend. "But how will we ever open this box?"

"You must journey once more to find the Great White Tiger," Lulu said. "The Snowkeeper will show you the way." She pointed to a small house on the mountainside below.

"I'm so sorry for the setback," Einstein said sadly.

"That's behind us now," Big Billy replied. "Remember, when we are together, we are strong."

"That's right!" Lulu said. "Be brave. Be loving. Be forgiving, if you want to be like the Great White Tiger. Good-bye now!"

With a flick of her tail, she was gone.

Big Billy steered the balloon toward the Snowkeeper's house. The adventure would continue.

Learn how Chattaboonga and her friends began their journey and met the Great White Tiger in Book One of the Gnoo Zoo series, *In Search of the Great White Tiger*.

In Book Two, *Chattaboonga's Chilling Choice*, the mischievous chimp would rather trust her instincts than the Great White Tiger's promises. She must learn the hard way that even when she is afraid, the Great White Tiger is always with the little band of travelers, and he will faithfully protect them on the journey.

In Gnoo Zoo Book Four, *Miss Marbles's Marvelous Makeover*, pride gets in the way of her wisdom and almost costs the vain ostrich her life. But the ever-gracious mercy of the Great White Tiger restores her to the group as they continue their important mission.

More Gnoo Zoo and Children of Faith products are coming soon!